A Rite to Kill

Wendy Adams was the island's top gardener. She had tremendous success with all types of plants. She even grew a lot of things that wisdom said would not grow there.

When asked how she managed to keep such healthy plants in that kind of insect-infested place she answered that she had almost a set of rites she always followed. It got rid of the pests very effectively.

Then a few pests died in her garden who were not insects, snails, mites, or mice.

Contents

Garden Party — pg. 1

Unwelcome Visitors — pg. 10

Eeny, Meeny, Miney, Mo — pg. 20

Another Pest Bites the Dust! — pg. 30

Wrong Place, Wrong Time — pg. 40

Another Garden Party — pg. 58

About the author

CD Moulton has traveled extensively over much of the world both in the music business, where he was a rock guitarist, songwriter and arranger and in an import/export business. He has been everything from a bar owner to auto salvage (junkyard) manager, longshoreman to high steel worker, orchid grower to landscaper, tropical fish farmer to commercial fisherman. He started writing books in 1983 and has published more than 350 books as of January 1, 2023. His most popular books to date are about research with orchids, though much of his science fiction and fantasy work has proven popular. He wrote the CD Grimes, PI series, and the Det. Nick Storie series, Clint Faraday series, and many other works.

He now resides in Gualaca, Chiriqui, Panamá, where he writes books, plays music with friends, does research with orchids and medicinal plants. He has lately become involved in fighting for the rights of the indigenous people, who are among his closest friends, and in fighting the extreme corruption in the courts and police in Panamá.

He offers the free e-book, *Fading Paradise*, that explains what he has been through because of the corruption.

CD is the discoverer of the Chadam Protocol for curing cancer.

Facebook page Ambrosia peruviana for cancer.

Garden Party

Wendy Adams carefully put on her latex gloves, checked the mixture of Parathion in her spray tank, checked the filer in her facemask, rechecked the mixture in the tank, put the Parathion 50% powder back in the lock cabinet, checked to be sure the syringe and atropine were there and not expired, closed the cabinet and locked the cabinet door, checked to be absolutely sure the lock was engaged, slipped on the plastic seal suit, and blew through the little tube she had as carefully glued onto the suit to be sure there was no leakage, picked up the tank, and marched to the row of camellias (that could not, theoretically, be grown on any tropical Caribbean island), and sprayed them carefully, covering the entire plant.

Parathion was outlawed fifty years ago, but her grandfather, who taught her how to grow plants, had four large packages of it in his shed. She used such very small amounts at one spraying that she still had more than one package left.

She had two hectares around her house on the island she had turned into an Eden. She grew a lot of things that simply couldn't be grown in that place. She had learned that many of that kind of thing could be grown if one would consider the overall balance they needed. Camellias needed cold to bloom, but she did manage to coax a few blooms each year from the more warmth tolerant varieties.

She very carefully checked to be sure she had covered the plants correctly, then turned on the bird repelling noise box. Birds would die in mere minutes around phosphorothioates. The sounds would continue for six hours, when the toxic properties would be low enough that no harm would come to birds.

She returned the sprayer and gear to the shed, decontaminated everything used, went through the shower with the contamination suit before opening it and taking it off. It was hot, but that was part of the deal. She disposed of the used cartridges from the gas mask and dropped the latex gloves into special trash bag, then sealed the bag.

There were a lot of those leaf cutting ants on the property next door that were starting to move underground onto her property. She prepared the cyanide bomb, and as carefully used it at the edge of her property. The Nelsons would probably allow her to get rid of the ants on their property if she asked, but, this way, she didn't have to ask. The gas would back up through the tunnels and get the whole colony. The Nelsons wouldn't be on this end of their property. It was just left there, full of weeds for almost two hundred meters.

Wendy sighed. It was eleven. The garden club would be there at three to hold their meeting, at which she would be the speaker. She wanted the place to be perfect.

She put the warning signs ten feet before the camellias and before the ant hill. No one would come here, but better to be safe.

The dahlias were blooming. They would soon give up the ghost. They were strictly annuals ,here in the tropics.

The many orchids, all species found in and on the Caribbean, were spectacular. That was a good thing about this time of year and parties. The show was magnificent!

February wasn't a good time, in most places, but it was a special time for flowers on the islands.

Uh-oh! There were saddlebacks on the hibiscus! The stinging caterpillars had to go ... but there wasn't time, now.

Wendy got a sign that warned people that there were stinging caterpillars on the hibiscus, then went in the house to prepare the snacks and such for the party. She was fortunate enough to have the schedules so well timed. She didn't have to rush around, like some. She took her time, and did it right, without a lot of confusion and tension. Consider what is to be done, make a plan, follow the plan. Very simple.

The khaki safari suit would be the thing, today. She didn't like to have to wear anything but her old faithful stained and worn blue jeans, but there were some British special guests of the Warrens. Wendy did like to impress people, and she knew how the English gardener was always portrayed.

Fix a light lunch. Relax for an hour. Bathe and dress. Set the tables. Gather her equipment, if any was needed, for the talk. Greet the guests. A sort of flow of things that would be smooth.

Would a big hat be too much? A tan straw hat with a big pink chin sash?

Yes. Definitely. Don't go so far they'll think you're insulting them. Make a joke about the costume. Maybe say that was what was in the movies, and she always wanted to have an excuse to wear it. She liked dressing up.

The Warrens came, and introduced their guests, the Stevens, from Hampton, England.

They were nice enough people, if just a little stuffy, at first. She figured it was how she was dressed, so made the story about always wanting an excuse to dress like that in her garden, particularly among the roses.

"Oh! That's right! Wendy grows *and blooms* hybrid tea roses, *here*!" Amy said. "She has camellias! *Here*!"

They all lightened up, and went onto the large terrace for fruit punch. The Andersons and the Mortons came next. They brought Sam Evans, a true pain in the ass pest. Then the Riveras, local bigshots, then the Bernstedts, then the Watkins. He was alright, but she was another pest. Ali Mendez and Jorge Hernandez. They were gay, but good people. Wanda Carstairs, the pest of pests, was with her latest "Good Friend," Jim Something. The Tompkins and the Reese's. Javier Lacrosse, a totally egotistical ass. Marty Feldman, a real gentleman, and a good friend. He was a botanist who liked to study her methods. Sandi Beech (she always thought of her as Sandi Bitch. She had to watch that she didn't make a Freudian slip) came with her aunt, Marta James, who said Sandi had turned down ten suitors so she could marry a man with a name like Beech. She would have settled for Klaus.

They finally started the meeting, and it was soon Wendy's turn. She was to talk about keeping pests and fungus out of her garden.

She talked for about fifteen minutes about the things she used, and warned, at each small step, that misuse of almost anything could do a great amount of harm – to the user as well as to the plants.

"I make a schedule that includes a check at every step. I call it my rites of care. It really is like a ritual, but, in the long run, saves both time and effort. The thing you must never forget is that you are working with poisons, in many instances.

"You have seen the signs where I say do not approach closer to the camellias. That's because I recently used a very powerful insecticide. By the ant hill, where we haven't gone today, there's a sign, because I used cyanide.

"Make a strict ritual and a schedule a part of the process. Take ridiculously unnecessary caution. *Not* getting poisoned or poisoning your plants is worth ten years of hindsight and 'I should have been more careful!' It could save the expense of a funeral, too. Yours. There is no such thing as too careful. It's a tired cliche, but better safe than sorry.

"You have to make choices. Many people can't understand why I can grow so many things so well, but it is a matter of my rites. If Parathion is the only thing we have that kills resistant star scale, you have to make a choice. The poison or the scale. My garden reflects that I have no scale.

"I also understand, fully, why most would not use the Parathion. It is outlawed most places, because it is so dangerous. My strongest rites are with its use.

"I hope I've covered everything. If there are any questions, please feel free to ask. The answers aren't going to suddenly come to you psychically."

There were a few questions, then the group ended the formal meeting and opted to sit around and chat, or go to the special parts of the gardens, where they asked Wendy how she managed to grow those things in the adverse conditions of a tropical island.

The party broke up as the sun was setting. The only ones who hung around were the pains in the asses. That was pretty much to be expected. After about fifteen minutes of having to put up with them, Marty came back to get his glasses, which he left on the table. He suggested that Wendy was probably tired, and would want to change into more comfortable clothes, so why not break it up and let her. They all acted surprised at what was so obvious, and apologized, then left. Wendy mouthed, "Thanks!" to Marty as he followed them out.

She had set it up so there wasn't much of anything left to do. The dishes and glasses were in a carton that she carried into the kitchen. She put the garbage in a bag, tied it, then put it in a can by the street, cleaned the dishes, wiped down the table, placed the chairs where they belonged, and folded the extras to put in the shed, then went in to take a luxurious bath and to watch a movie on TV that soon bored her, so she went to bed, where she finished the murder mystery she was reading. It was written by a California lawyer, and tended to a lot of courtroom dialogue. It was just short of boring, so she soon turned out the light and went to sleep. Tomorrow, another round of getting rid of the pests. It was neverending. Mice were ruining too many things, tearing down the plants to get to the seeds.

She wished they didn't smell so when they were poisoned. She would put out a dozen or so traps. It would take about three days to get rid of those.

Then there were other pests, some just the annoying kind that she was determined to get out of her garden.

"Wendy! We've been here in this paradise landscape looking at some of the fantastic things you have!

"Sandi and Javier were showing us the roses. I've never seen such healthy plants, and the blooms are just out of this world!" Samantha Stevens cried. "They know all your secrets! They're not secrets anymore!"

Wendy smiled. "I don't have any secrets, but I'm glad you can use the information, though I doubt it will be useful in England."

"Yes. We have the perfect conditions for roses, but yours put ours to shame, and in a place where they shouldn't be surviving, at all," William Stevens said. "You are an amazing person!"

"Why, how flattering! Please don't stop!

"It's really all done with logic. Roses are heavy feeders. It's the same with you and me. If other conditions are causing us distress, we can usually change our diets to compensate. There's no rest period for roses, here, which is the major pitfall. They don't get the period where they harden up, which is when they bloom their best. I add a lot of potassium to the fertilizer for three onths to compensate. It will hardens them, chemically. More heat, so more phosphorus. Reduce the nitrogen so they don't try to grow and harden at the same time.

"I was setting mouse traps. They're a problem, here. Would you like some tea? I only have the green tea, which I like."

"I prefer the green tea," Javier said. "It's healthy and flavorful. It's always my choice!"

Like we care? Wendy thought.

"Well, sit! I'll boil water. Sugar and cream or lemon?"

"Don't boil the tea!" Sandi warned.

"Of course not! What idiot would boil tea?" Wendy asked. "Just a few minutes."

She went inside to put a pot of water on, and took cups and saucers and the spoons, tea, cream, and sugar to place on the table. They chatted, and drank the tea, then Wendy showed them around the garden. She came to the sign that said there were stinging caterpillars on the hibiscus, and slapped her head. "I never forget, but I did!"

"Well, you had a lot to do, yesterday," Javier said. "I'll come over and spray them for you this afternoon. Shouldn't use those sprays in the heat of the day!"

"Oh, I'll spray them. It's no trouble," Wendy answered. "You have to use a gas mask with the stuff. Temix. And a suit and gloves."

"I insist! It's no trouble. Gives me something to do! Five o'clock, I'll be here! I insist!"

"Well ... all right. Thank you." *For showing off to these people, you asshole!* was added in her mind.

They talked a bit more, then Javier and the Stevens left. Sandi hung around.

"I didn't mean to insult you about the tea," she said. "It was only a suggestion. A lot of people boil tea, and it turns slimy and sour."

"I didn't mean to sound catty," Wendy replied. "I have a headache from something, and I tend to be a bit of an ass when I'm like that. I take things the wrong way."

"Oh. I'm like that. If I don't feel good I take it out on the nearest victim.

"I have some acetaminophen."

"No. I have some willows by the pond. I chew the stem, and get natural aspirin. I try to always use natural things for medicines. No side effects. Sometimes the side effects are worse than what you take the stuff for."

"Yeah. Well, I'll get along home. Thanks for everything." She waved, and left.

Sandi Bitch! You did that deliberately, you cheap whore! She went in the house, then to the shed to check that she had the Temix and such, then went into the little town, two miles along the island road. She had to remember to have the oil checked. It was about time to change it. She did some shopping, and was just going to the garage for the oil change when Javier came by. He waved, and said he was on the way to her place. Would she be long?

"The keys to the shed are under the lamp on the terrace. Everything you need is in the shed. Remember to lock it. There are gloves in a box on the shelf to the right, and I've mixed the Temix. It's in the sprayer. Throw the gloves in the little toxic garbage bag when you're through, please. I don't ever want anything around if the neighborhood kids come through. They'd pick up the gloves and play with them."

He agreed, and went on. She found she would have to wait half an hour for the oil change. She went to the café for some Orange/pineapple/banana chicha. It took more than an hour, but she headed back home. Javier's car was sitting out front. He'd supposedly done the spraying, and would be hanging around to aggravate her.

She sighed. She could hope not!

Sandi Beech left that sweet-tongued snake's party after feeling her out as to why she came on so damned strong about the goddamned tea. Maybe she did have a headache. She'd been using all those chemicals.

Javier was coming over to spray Temix. The stuff was dangerous. Artie wouldn't let her use it, at all.

Arthur Beech. She'd fallen in love with him, and made a cutesy about her new name. Her mother had glommed onto it, and kept saying she waited for someone with a name like that. She wished she'd never said it, and that her mother would shut the hell up!

She was in a terrible mood. She was going to show the Stevens Wendy's place, and that Javier asshole had come along and invited himself. Ed and Hariette Warren had to go to work – they were the teachers and everything else at the only school on the island – so she had volunteered to show their English guests around. Javier, as was his greatest talent, managed to insert himself so he could show how much more he knew about everything than anybody.

She hated the little scheming toad. She sort of hoped there would be an accident with the Temix, where he would be the pest that was eliminated. Wendy had Temix and Parathion and cyanide in that shed she kept locked up like a bank vault – then showed everyone where the keys were if they needed anything when she wasn't home. Take all that great precaution when you use the stuff so there is no contact, then let anyone go into the place where she kept the stuff. Stupid cow!

Well, the day's plan was screwed up, anyhow. She might as well work in her own garden. Maybe it would calm her down some. Those cutter ants were coming into her place. Wendy used cyanide gas. She had canisters of the stuff in her shed. Artie wouldn't allow her to use it, but he was at work. It was the only thing that was really effective against those ants.

It would take her about ten minutes to drive to Wendy's and back. Artie would never know.

She drove to Wendy's, and went to the shed. The keys were under the lamp. Three locks on the door, and put the keys there for anyone who came along. Stupid as dirt!

The Temix was laid on the shelf, along with gloves, a plastic raincoat thing, and a gas mask with a new canister for the wet filter.

That was a clever thing, invented by Wendy's grandfather. It was a porous carbon air filter with a canister in front that had a solution that would dissolve most poisonous gases before they got to the activated charcoal. Double-safe!

The cyanide was in the little cabinet with the extra lock and the red danger sign on the door, along with a skull and crossbones. This padlock key.

Javier Lacrosse had a purpose. He was doing everything he could think of to get close to Wendy Adams. Including coming out here to spray her miserable caterpillars.

He was used to a good life. A good life costs money. He was getting far too low on money. Wendy Adams had control of a lot of money. He was determined to get that money.

His plan was to marry her. On this island, he couldn't inherit for two years, then everything was community property that wasn't under a corporate name. Two years of bliss, then she would have a fatal accident, and Javier Lacrosse would be set for the life he was determined to have.

He sometimes sensed that Wendy was one of those people who projected a happy front, but who are ice-cold, inside. He sensed her standoffishness, at times. He would have to thaw her out. He was French, which was, according to his father, enough to let him have any woman he wanted.

He didn't want Wendy, but he needed her. Temporarily.

Let's see. Latex gloves, sprayer (he actually was scared shitless of these kinds of absorbable poisons) plastic raincoat (in this heat, yet!), and gas mask.

Weird looking thing. Her grandfather invented it. Why the hell didn't he take out a patent? There was a million dollars, right here in his hand. *He* was certainly going to patent it!

Let's see. Carry the crap out to the hibiscus, slip on the raincoat and hood, put on the gloves. Now the gas mask. Pop it over your head and ... damn! No air is coming through! What the hell?

Oh. Moist canister. Pull the tab to open the air passage through the ... what is that smel...?

Wanda Carstairs saw Sandi leave the shed and take something to her car. Probably something for her garden.

She was there to get something from the shed. She had tried to grow a Marechal Neil rose for years, and had followed Wendy's advice in doing it. Her plant was doing well enough, but it simply refused to bloom. Wendy had said she forced a rest with potassium fertilizer. She would have it mixed and marked. Wanda Carstairs was about to have as much success with a rose as Wendy Adams did!

Now! The keys. There's a lot of stuff on the shelf. A sprayer and all that poison safety stuff. She was going to spray something ... the sign by the hibiscus. Stinging worms. That's probably Temix. That's also probably why all the stuff. That fancy gas mask Wendy's father or someone invented. It had been explained in tedious detail how it worked.

Maybe it was worth the trouble. Who knows? Maybe the stuff in the canister would poison you first. Sometimes those kinds of poisons didn't show effects for years.

Where would the fertilizer be? All the cabinets were locked, then the keys to all of them were over the shelf by the door.

Well, it was to keep kids safe, not people who knew about the poisons.

Nothing but sharp tools in this one.

Poison gas in this one. Would that mask thing stop it?

Yes. It was made for that kind of thing. Just don't use a poison gas canister instead of the safety canister.

Here it is. Vegetable: acid, vegetable: alkaline, General foliage plants, rose grow special, rose rest special. That's it! She has a ton of the stuff. She won't miss a couple of pounds.

Did I put the lock back on that gas cabinet ... glad I checked! I didn't click it locked. She would know someone was in here.

Now to make my great escape from the scene of the crime!

Wanda giggled, and left. There would be no sign she was ever there.

Maybe fingerprints, but who would look for those?

Wendy parked the car in the port, and carried stuff inside. Javier wasn't there, so he must be out in the garden. Maybe at the shed.

She went to the shed, but it was locked tight, and the keys were returned to the lamp.

She went out to the hibiscus. Javier was laying there. He hadn't sprayed anything yet. The tab from the gas mask was in his hand. He was obviously dead. His face was blue.

She squealed, and ran back to the phone. She called the police, spoke to a Captain Zayle, and was told to not let anyone near the area.

"I can't see how it was possible. The canisters are nothing alike!" Wendy cried. "The gas mask canisters aren't kept anywhere near the cyanide canisters!"

"They're about the same size. It was a clever way to rig it. It was no accident. It was murder," Captain Martin Zayle, island police force, said. "The cyanide canister was put into the mask, sort of like it was jammed. A tube with the seal over it. Put on the mask and pull the seal, cyanide gas at high pressure, dead in seconds."

Wendy shuddered.

"So. Who knew he was going to be here and would use the mask?"

"Nobody. Me ... and Sandi Beech, and the Stevens. They're from England, and didn't know him except from this morning. Maybe they met at the garden party, yesterday."

"Who knew the hibiscus were to be sprayed today with that extreme poison?"

"Everybody at the party. I had a sign ... right there by Javier's body."

"So it could have been meant for you."

Wendy's eyes flew open wide. She gasped. "I never considered ... I never even thought ... It ... oh, my god!"

"I think we'll have to find this killer, fast. If Lacrosse was the wrong victim, the killer will try again."

Wendy whimpered.

"Do you have any enemies who might do something like that?"

"No. I have a few people I don't much like, but not that I'd kill! I suppose ... I didn't like Javier. He was a phony asshole, but that doesn't mean I'd kill him! I don't like Sandi, Wanda Carstairs, or Sam Evans. I'm neutral about most people. I particularly like Marty Feldman, and the Warrens, and the Watkins.

"Don't tell anyone. I always try to act like I'm everybody's friend, but I'm not, really. The only one who may know I don't like her is Sandi Beech. She dosen't like me, either. We try to act civilized when we're around each other."

"You'll have to watch your back until we know more."

"Don't I know it!"

"Tell me what you can about the ones you don't like, and who may not like you. Maybe we can connect something.

"There's Sandi, as stated. Sam Evans is a bit of a type who...."

Samuel Taylor Evans stared at Wanda Carstairs. "Are you saying that Javier phony asshole is dead? From some kind of insecticide poisoning?"

"Yes! I just came from town, and that police car was in front of her place, and Javier's car was sitting there, and I asked Johnny Mercer, he's the one who helps Zayle when he needs it, what was going on. Dr. Plant was there. He said Javier had gotten a snoutful of cyanide, some-how, and was dead as a doorknob."

"Weird. I always said sooner or later Adams' poison chest was going to kill the wrong thing. It was a joke when I said there were some human pests around here that could maybe use a big helping of that Parathion stuff. Javier was the top pest I was talking about.

"I guess Wendy will take it in stride. She always does."

"I envy her ability to stay calm and strong, no matter what.

"Javier was a bit of a pest, but not near as bad as Marty Feldman. I always think he's trying to get into my pants. He has a sort of subliminal signal of some sort.

"Well, I'll go on home. We can wait to see what happens." She went out the gate, and got in her car. Sam looked thoughtful.

Sam Evans couldn't accept that this thing was accidental. Javier was the kind of person people automatically disliked. He was, as Wanda noted, phony. You knew it, instinctively. He thought he was some kind of dream lover, or something. If Wanda had said *he* was trying to get into her pants, he would have had to agree. He was the type who would try with every woman he met, but who almost always struck out. In his own mind, he probably thought he hadn't wanted the woman who turned him down. It was almost sickening the way he put on an overdone French accent whenever he met a new woman.

He was also the type who never did a favor for anyone without a reason. Sure as Sunday, he had some kind of sordid ulterior motive when he volunteered to spray those hibiscus. Everyone knew he was afraid of those poisons.

Sam Evans might be able to get in closer with Wendy, now that this had happened. She seemed ready to help anyone, and did give advice that worked wonders. He was sure she left little details out. His own orchids had improved a hundred ten percent since he followed her advice, but she had those high altitude types that she was growing, here, at three hundred meters elevation. He could keep them alive with what she taught him, but he couldn't make them look happy.

All her plants looked happy. If he could manage to hang around, he was sure he could figure out a few of her secrets. Maybe he would go over there in the morning and sympathize with her. It was worth a try!

Wanda left Sam, and worried. She had been in that shed, and had seen the poison stuff laid out for Javier. She had joked to herself about leaving fingerprints, but maybe that Capt. Zayle would look for prints, there. He was pretty sharp. Her fingerprints were even on that cabinet where the poisons were kept! How could she be so damned *stupid,* sometimes!?

She would go to Wendy in the morning, and tell her about it. Wendy wouldn't mind. She said a lot of times that people could have whatever they needed. She could just claim the Stevens had reminded her about her roses. She went over there, Wendy wasn't home, so she did what Wendy herself said to do. She got a little of the rose fertilizer. After all, that's what she did!

It would work out. She did have an explanation for having been in that shed.

She couldn't work up enough emotion about dear old Javier, the overdone French creep, to give a damn. One less garden pest.

Things would work out. They always did.

Sandi Beech heard the news that Javier was dead. She was glad she was on the phone, because she wouldn't be able to explain her little gleeful smirk. If anyone ever deserved what Doc had called a snout full of cyanide, it was that snake.

She'd fallen for his line when he first came to the island. While he never actually said anything like blackmail, he wouldn't hesitate. He'd gotten a "loan" from her for two hundred dollars, just two weeks ago. He had hinted that he needed the money, and would rather get it from her than from her husband.

Zayle would probably check for fingerprints in the shed, but she'd been there when Wendy was with her, and could expect them and everybody elses' on the island, for that matter. She was sure there were none inside the cabinet. All she'd touched at all was the canister she took.

Marty Feldman heard about the death, and immediately went to console Wendy. He cared a lot for her, in a brotherly sort of way. This kind of thing could be hard on a person, and she wasn't as strong as the front she put up.

She was worried that the poison might have been intended for her. He couldn't argue the possibility. After all, it was put in her gas mask, and very few knew Javier would be using it.

He insisted she move to his place. Just for a week, or until they found who did this. She would damned well be safe, there!

Zayle agreed. There might be another trap of some kind already there on her place.

Bert Watkins hung up the phone and turned to Emily to say, "That was Ed Warren. He says Javier Lacrosse was murdered in Wendy's garden, a couple of hours ago. Hariette is afraid it was something put there to kill Wendy. Cyanide in a gas mask. It didn't make any sense. A gas mask would neutralize cyanide, I'd think."

"You know how Hariette gets things twisted up. Maybe she meant that there was cyanide, and he wasn't wearing the mask, or something. I'll talk to Doc tomorrow, and find out what really happened.

"I always worried about those poisons. Wendy is all gung-ho for the natural medicines and less chemicals on vegetables, then she uses all of them in her own garden.

"We'll find out about it in the morning. The real story."

"At least, it couldn't have happened to a more deserving person than Lacrosse! He was one phony bastard if there ever was one!"

"Bert! Really! Don't speak ill of the dead!"

"There's nothing else I can speak about that one!"

Martin Zayle looked around the shed. Adams certainly went to extremes to use those things safely. Everything was locked.

He took out his fingerprint kit. He wasn't going to look in the obvious places. Anyone on the island had a reason to have prints in that shed.

He found the keys to the lockers on the ring above the shelf, where Wendy said they'd be. He slipped on the latex gloves and took the ring to the potting bench to carefully dust them all, saving the prints found with the Scotch Tape. He then tried them, to find the locks they fit. The one from the poison cabinet had several sets, one atop the other. Only the last user was clear, though the one before that had enough to identify. He could easily tell those two were put there since Wendy had used the key. Her prints were easy to identify, because of a scar across the index finger and a strange whorl pattern.

He had dusted the cyanide container in the mask. Nothing. Gloves. He could hope the gloves were used when the canister was forced into the mask, and not before.

He opened the cabinet to look inside. The only prints there that were important were on the removed canister, so it wouldn't prove anything to waste time with that.

The prints on the cabinet key weren't on other keys, except for the top one. The keys were on the ring in the order of the cabinets. The top print was on three keys. The first was a tool cabinet, then the poisonous chemicals cabinet, then the fertilizer cabinet.

He opened the fertilizer cabinet and looked over the clearly marked bins of fertilizer. He saw some spillage by the rose rest fertilizer, so dusted the cover. The print was there.

More than seventy five percent that the second print on that poison cabinet key was their killer.

Now to find who left it there.

Wendy went over things in her mind, again, very carefully.

Had she covered all of it? Had she left out that one little thing that would allow Zayle to solve it?

Zayle thought she was the one the cyanide was meant for. That was clear. He thought she was in danger.

This was a scary kind of thing. She knew very damned well Zayle had to consider her a prime suspect, but the person most in danger if she didn't do it. That meant he would have to tread very carefully along either path, in case he was wrong.

Had she left out anything? She tried to get it all straightened out to where Zayle would see that she was the one in danger. He must concentrate on protecting her. That was the most important thing to her, at the moment. He must be certain of her innocence.

Bert and Emily were just leaving. It was very considerate of them to come to offer their help, at a time like this. They were thoughtful people.

Zayle came around from the back to ask if any of the neighbors came onto the property except through the front gates. She said she didn't know. She supposed they could. He said there was evidence of someone coming through the weed field to the north. It was a steep drop in back to the ocean. An experienced climber could possibly come that way, but it wasn't likely.

"Especially seeing they can come and go as they please through the front."

He grinned, and said it was his job to check out all the possibilities, weak or strong. He went toward the southern border, and she went back inside. A few minutes later, Sam Evans came up the path. She sighed, and went to greet him. This was something she would have to put up with.

He had a spiel about hanging around to protect her. He had been on a nearby island the whole day, yesterday, so couldn't have possibly been the one to have arranged the poisoning, and he wasn't going to take "No" for an answer.

She said he could hang around, but she thought it was a waste of his time.

She knew full well he only wanted to learn her deepest "secrets" about growing things. She didn't have any. If these people would do all the things she suggested, they would have as good luck, but they never did. They took little shortcuts that made something positive into a failure.

What the hell! She could use a bit of help in clearing that section in the back corner. It was a stand of cedar trees that had a lot of brush to clear out, then could be made into an orchid garden. Evans' specialty was orchids. It would work out very well.

"Well, I was planning on clearing out a place for the new intermediate orchids on the back end, today. It's a lot of work, but I think it should make a very nice little addition."

"It will be perfect!" he replied. "I want to see just how you prepare those places. I have a bunch of old cedars on a piece of my place where I was planning on making into an orchid garden. Maybe put a little wrought iron and glass table in the clearing ... which would be a bad idea. It would be in the full sun!

"Just being here makes me see where I'm apt to do the wrong thing, without thinking it through."

"Wrought iron is decorative and pretty, but is uncomfortable as hell! It takes a lot of upkeep. You can get some very nice plastic items that're both comfortable and maintenance free. Be practical. Making a fancy show is okay for a few special occasions, but useless for what you want. Everyday relaxation among your plants."

"You're right. I was planning a place for parties, more than for practical use. I never have parties, so it was a stupid thing to think about. I was raised on 'impress the Joneses', and can't seem to break out of that way of thinking."

She told Zayle they were going to be on the lower end, on the point, if he needed her for anything. He said he was about through, and would call, if he needed more. She could carry her cell phone with her. She got machetes and an ax from the shed, and they went to start the project. He asked if it was too soon after the tragedy, but she assured him working was the only way to get it off her mind. She'd go crazy, sitting around thinking.

They worked for about two hours, and had a
good bit of the copse cleared just the way she
wanted. She had room to move around wherever
she liked, but had left a lot of closer shrubs to
give heavier shade to certain spots. Sam said
they should clear all the shrubbery. She argued
that would leave her without a place for a dozen
varieties of orchids that required just that kind
of situation. She wanted to use as few limits to
the plants as possible, even if that meant more
limits to her. He thought about it, and agreed.
He would clear away too much, and the plants
wouldn't thrive. He would think someone didn't
tell him the right way. She made him see that he
would have failed to follow her advice all the
way.

He wouldn't go close to the edge of the drop-
off to the ocean, and kept cautioning her about
it. She said it was solid rock, and she wasn't
afraid of heights, anyhow. She stayed about a
meter back from the edge, in case of loose rock
that wouldn't hold her weight. She had slipped
at one spot, but there was plenty of overhanging
branches on the cedars. She grabbed on, and
went on. He shook his head and rolled his eyes.
He said he thought she was a goner. He almost
had a heart attack!

"I don't go that close when there aren't things to grab if you slip. That would be stupid. It's almost a hundred meters, straight down!"

She said she was going to the house to fix them some lunch. She hoped he liked Itallian meatball sandwiches, because she had fixed the sauce last night, and had bought the Cuban bread. He said he'd rake the small branches laying around into a pile and put them in sacks to throw onto the compost pile. He loved meatball sandwiches.

She returned, twenty minutes later. Evans was nowhere to be seen. He hadn't gone back the path to the house. She would have seen him.

She called, and got no answer. She went around among the cedars, but found nothing, until a small spot where there was what appeared to be blood on a branch. The ground was disturbed near the spot. It was right at the edge of the precipice.

She drew a deep breath, and went to look over the edge. She could see Evans' body on the rocks by the water. There was a bloody machete a few meters below, caught in the ferns growing on the rocks.

She took out her cell phone to call Zayle.

Martin Zayle looked at the blood on the cedar branch. He looked over the edge. The police boat was just coming around the point, and would retrieve the body, after taking a full set of photos and doing a video that would include everything.

He studied the cedar copse, carefully. Wendy was standing there, waiting.

"Okay. You were clearing the underbrush, and had gotten everything cleared, except that piece by the edge. You went back to the house to make some sandwiches. You got back here, and he wasn't anywhere around. You saw the blood on the branch, and looked over. There he was.

"That about it?"

"Yes."

"Okay. It looks like he was cutting the smaller branches low, and slipped on the loose rock here. Maybe he got a foot tangled in the vines...."

There was a call from below. Doc yelled that there were no cuts on the body. There was a Pitt Bull with its head cut almost off, in the water.

"The dogs?" Wendy said. "They're the Connors' dogs. They're the only ones around. They don't bother anyone."

"So one attacked Evans when he was by the edge. He was using the machete, cut the dog, and they both went over."

"No. He wouldn't go near the edge. He was afraid."

"What?"

"He kept warning me not to go to the edge. He wouldn't get any closer than six or eight feet. I slipped once, and he almost had a heart attack! I always stay where I can grab the overhanging branches, and wouldn't have dropped far enough to hurt me there, anyhow. I'm not stupid."

Zayle made a grimace. "Maybe telling me that was stupid? Now I know it was murder."

"You did, anyhow."

He nodded, and said, "Come along. I want to show you something. If no one came from the house path, there's only one other place where they could have come." He led her to a section on the weedy lot next door, and to an animal path through the tangled briars and tall weeds and scrub. There was a rotted limb laying toward the side.

"Here. I pushed that rotten bush over to where it was across the path, like it had fallen. Someone had to shove it over there. Now for the next part."

He went to the narrow path between a tree trunk and a large boulder. There was old straw covering the ground. Zayle carefully moved the straw aside, revealing a soft sandy patch with a partial footprint.

"I'll be damned! A woman's shoe!" he cried. "It's one of those semi-platform things."

Wendy could see the print. It was about three quarters from the heel to where it was off the sandy patch. It was the middle of the ball of the foot to the heel and was distinctively a platform shape.

He took a package of white powder from his case and a bottle of water and a bowl. He mixed the plaster of Paris and made a cast of the print. They chatted about incidentals while they waited for it to set, then he replaced the straw, and they went back to the cedar copse. Mario Arauz, a local teenage boy, was there, tying a rope around a tree trunk. He would lower himself down to retrieve the machete. He slipped on latex gloves before he went over the side. He was back up, two minutes later, with the machete. A glance at the bloody thing showed there were no prints. Zayle gave Mario five dollars, and he took his rope and left.

"You told me Evans was a pest, and you said Lacrosse was a pest. Somebody's taking pest control a little too far."

"I hope you don't think it was me!"

"No way! Whoever slashed that dog had blood spatter on that branch. There would be a lot more than that little bit on the one who made the cut. That blood was still dripping wet. You wouldn't have had time to change clothes from the time the cut was made until I got here. You could have worn a raincoat, but you wouldn't have time to dispose of it. Raincoat or not, there would be blood on your arms and hands, though I imagine the killer was wearing gloves. If not, someone will have some explaining to do about why their prints are on that machete – which they aren't."

"I wish you had a lot of officers. You could have one go to every suspect before they had a chance to clean up."

"I wish a lot of things. Ain't gonna happen!"

"Let's go back to the house, or something. I want to be away from here. I feel like I'm standing here with a scope sight with the cross-hairs on my heart!"

"Probably closer to the truth than you'll want to think about."

Wanda Carstairs watched as that Capt. Zayle got out of his car and went along the path behind Wendy's house. Wendy would be back at the copse, with Sam. He said he was going to insist she let him be with her until the Javier death thing was settled somehow.

She felt like a sneak, always waiting until no one was around to get things from the shed. Wendy would tell her to help herself, but she could sense that Wendy didn't really like her.

All she wanted was a little of that blood and bone meal mix for her roses. Wendy had a hundred pound bag of it that she'd only used a pound or two of.

She went to the shed, and was almost shocked that it was unlocked. Wendy must be a lot more disturbed than she was letting on.

She pushed the door open and stepped inside.

What?! There was someon....

Marty Feldman came to the house as Zayle and Wendy came from the far side. Mario Arauz was just getting on his scooter, and they had waved at each other.

What was going on? He would have to find out if Zayle had found any clues.

Zayle had a machete in a plastic wrap in one hand and a bunch of light tools in the other. There was blood on the machete. Wendy had a paper sack in one hand and a hoe and rake in the other. He asked what she had in the paper bag, and if it could hope to top a bloody machete.

"My god!" she cried. "I've been carrying these sandwiches around, and didn't even realize it!"

Marty saw he was right. All this had affected Wendy a lot more than she would let on.

"We can eat the damned sandwiches," Zayle said. "It's a damned certain bet Evans won't be dining."

"Sam?" Marty asked. "Don't tell me that Sam was where that machete got.... What in *hell* is going on here!"

"I wish I knew," Zayle answered. "There's too much that doesn't make much sense. I checked everyone, as far as I could. There's no connection I can see between Lacrosse and Evans. They were never anywhere near the same place at the same time before coming here. There isn't that kind of connection with anyone in your group, except the Warrens and the Watkins, who were from the same state, at least, if different ends of it."

"I knew Wanda Carstairs from a trip to the Bahamas, a few years ago. We wrote each other an e-mail or two, then she showed up here, with her husband, Phil. I'd met him on that same trip," Marty offered . "I knew Wendy from the Orchid Society Convention in San Francisco. I told her about this place."

"I knew Marty and Ed Warren. I'd never met any of the others before I moved here," Wendy said.

"Oh? You didn't know Sandi Beech before she married Arthur? When she was Sandi James?" Zayle asked.

"No. Should I have?"

"She lived in Temple Terrace for two years. You lived in Brandon for one of the same years."

"Both Tampa area," Wendy agreed. "I never met her. There were about two million other people in the area I didn't meet.

"Sorry. I'm scared by this, even though whoever it is didn't kill Sam by mistake. I have to worry about being part of something I don't know anything about."

"You learned a lot about all of us with your police network, I suppose," Marty said. "If there was no connection before, it has to be something from here. Other than the fact they were both annoying people, I can't think what it could be."

"Would it be that Lacrosse was trying to blackmail people, and Evans knew about it?" Zayle asked.

"What?! *Blackmail*!" Marty cried.

"Yes. When I checked his place, there were several things that could possibly be used in blackmail. Pictures of him in a compromising situation with a couple of your group."

"Who?" Wendy asked.

"I would never reveal that. I'll just destroy the photos and papers as soon as I determine that they have nothing to do with this. The blackmail wouldn't be because of legal matters. They were personal things."

Wendy looked thoughtful. "I know there was nothing about me in that kind of thing. I haven't been in any compromising situations with anyone here – damn it! Marty's life is an open book. Wanda isn't the type who would pay blackmail. Everyone knows she strays when Phil's not around. Sandi, I would assume there have to be fifty things she could be blackmailed for.

"I'm sorry. I always call her Sandi Bitch. She's catty and sneaky, so I tend to stretch that a little. A lot, really. We pretend that we don't despise each other, and try to keep distance between us."

"Well, let's put this stuff in the shed, and I was serious about the sandwiches," Marty suggested.

"We can eat them here, on the terrace. The shed can wait. For once in my life, I'm not obsessing about that shed."

The sat at the glass-top table to eat the delicious sandwiches, then Marty said he would go back home. This was all beyond him. Zayle grabbed the tools, and said the machete could stay there for five minutes, then he would take it to his, excuse the exaggeration, lab.

He and Wendy went around and down the path to the shed. Wanda Carstairs was laying half inside and half out. There was blood every-where. It looked like her throat had been cut!

Wendy said, "Oh, god!" staggered, then sat hard on the ground, shaking her head.

"I will not faint! I am stronger than that! I will *not* faint!" she wailed.

Zayle used his phone. Doc was just getting to the ambulance (of sorts) with Evans' body. He said it was half a kilometer. He'd be right there.

Zayle carefully stepped over Wanda, and slipped on latex gloves from the box on the shelf. There was a bloody sickle laying on the potting bench.

"It's supposed to look like you did it," Zayle decided. "We're supposed to think anyone else would have dropped the sickle, or taken it with them. You would put it where you could clean it off and return it to its proper hanger spot. Only you would be so choosy about this shed and the tools.

"They missed one tiny little detail."

"What?"

"You were with me. I checked this shed on my way in, when you called. She wasn't there, so she was killed after I went to the point. You were there, and I was with you every second, until now.

"They missed one other little thing."

"Which is?"

"The key to the lock on the door is hanging in the padlock. No one has touched that since the killer opened the door.

"What was Wanda doing here?"

"I imagine she was getting some rose fertilizer. I make special mixes, and everyone uses them." She went to the shed and around, leaning over Wanda's body, while holding onto the jamb.

"Martin, the raincoat's gone!"

"Raincoat?"

"Yes. I use it when I use the toxic sprays. It hangs right on that cabinet door. It's gone!

"Martin! Look!"

There was a bloody shoe print on the doorsill, close to Wanda's body. It was a complete print of a platform shoe, exactly like the one in the sand.

"So. It was her!" Wendy said.

"Her?"

"Sandi Beech. She and Wanda were the only ones in the group who wear the things. There's no blood on the bottoms of Wanda's shoes, so that leaves Sandi Bitch!"

Zayle nodded. "Then it'll be her print on that key and on the others. She probably got the raincoat ... then why was she back...?

"Wendy, she came earlier to get the raincoat to use when she killed the dog. She was bringing it *back* here, rinsed clean, when she saw Wanda coming for some fertilizer, and saw her in the shed. She probably saw Wanda coming just as she was coming out, and went inside to put on the raincoat, and grabbed the sickle. If we can find where she got rid of the raincoat, we'll have her another way. Bet the farm on it!"

They waited for Doc, then went into the little town, where Zayle made out a warrant form for Sandi Beech, her possessions, with most direction on shoes, and to allow fingerprinting. This wasn't the states. She couldn't refuse. Technically, he didn't even need the warrant, here.

"Ken will be royally pissed when I break up his siesta to have him sign a warrant I don't really need." Kenneth Darling was the closest thing they had to a judge. "I wish she'd forgotten to wipe the damned keys this time!" His kit showed the prints had been wiped off the keys to the shed. "Maybe those from last time will do."

They were just leaving Darling's place when they spotted Sandi going into the market. It was a small place that sold everything from dog food to filet mignon, from needles to axes, from socks to Tuxedos. (Well, that part's an exaggeration. Nobody would ever wear a tuxedo on that island, for any reason.) They went to her, and asked why she was wearing flip-flops, when she generally wouldn't be caught dead wearing them.

"The sole came off my plats. I need new ones. I lost my other pair, three days ago, at the beach. They were right by my towel, and were gone when I got out of the water. I should buy three or four pairs, so they'll be there when something happens to a pair."

"You lost them two days ago?" Zayle asked.

"Yeah. I was with Emily Warren, we went swimming, and they were gone when I got out of the water. I didn't notice 'til I got to my car, and they weren't there. I went back to the beach, but they weren't there, either."

"So Emily will know," Wendy said.

Sandi shrugged. "She might. She went to her car and saw me going back to the beach. I called that I left some things."

Zayle shrugged. He and Wendy went outside, where he cursed, colorfully. "I'll still have those prints from the key. She'll say she'd been there before, and her prints would naturally be on them. Damn! She'll have gotten rid of the shoes."

They drove to Emily and Ed's place. Emily said Sandi had left her sunglasses, or something, and went back for them. She wasn't sure just what it was.

"So. She had phenomenal luck! She actually left her glasses, by mistake, and Emily saw her going back to get something she left on the beach," Zayle complained. "We'll play holy hell proving anything else.

"I wonder why she's killing people off. If we can find it, we have motive, then the rest will be corroborating evidence.

"Besides the fact people didn't like her, do you know anything solid?"

"Not really. I wonder if she's just a homicidal maniac! If that's the case, I'm never going to be out of danger, so long as she's alive and free! If we don't know what sets her off, nobody's safe!"

"We'll have to find the motive. That's all there is to it. I can't do a thing with what I have."

They went back to the station, such as it was, where Zayle would catalogue all the evidence he had. Wendy headed for home. She was deeply worried about this thing!

Sandi watched Wendy and that handsome cop walk out of the market, and smirked. They knew damned well she'd gotten rid of those pests and snakes! They also knew they didn't have the chance of a candle in a hurricane of proving it.

Except Wanda. Wanda was a pain in the ass, but not the kind who would ever blackmail anyone. It was too bad she came just at that moment. She was coming up the path to the shed when Sandi had just brought the raincoat back, sparkling clean, like that stlly damned obsessive nutcase, Wendy, always kept everything.

She'd put the raincoat in a tin can full of rocks and thrown it into the south current. It would be miles away, by now.

It was plain dumb luck that she'd dropped her sunglasses on the way back to her car the other day, and that Emily had seen her going back to get something she left. Emily drove away. Now she would remember that Sandi Beech had lost something on the beach, and wouldn't be able to say what it was.

Maybe she would get rid of Wendy. What the hell! She'd gotten rid of the other drags on her life. Wendy didn't like her, and she didn't like Wendy. It was easy, as she'd proven. It was really fun, in a way. She was smarter than any of them. She was so far ahead of them, they knew she was the one knocking those crumby bastards off, and they knew they couldn't prove it. She'd learned another little thing or two with each one. She would never be caught to where they could even bring a charge.

It really was a thrill. Sort of fun. It was even fun when she cut that dog's head off. The blood spurting and the dog running right off the edge.

Evans was the easiest. It took a lot of planning and thought to rig that cyanide canister for the French poodle, as she called him. Evans, all she did was get him to come close to the edge to help her lift a log there, hit him with a rock, and push him over the side.

Well, she fooled them just enough, this time. She could fool them anytime. It was a game, really, and she was winning. She wouldn't stop winning. She could outsmart the whole crowd of idiots. They didn't have a brain, combined!

Maybe she'd get rid of Marty Feldman, next. She could sense that he had some kind of problem with her. He was a little smarter than the others, so maybe he should go. Better to not take any chances. He might be able to find a way to trip her up. He was clever.

Who else? She was on a roll, so ride the crest! Get things the way she wanted them. If that meant getting rid of ... distractions, why not?

The first one was hard. That was the Collins girl, who called her a cheap whore in front of all her friends, because she took ... Frankie, was his name. She took him to bed, just for fun. She wasn't interested in keeping him, for Christ's sake! It was one night.

Her, she pushed in front of a car. She was scared, but it was a thrill. It was five years before she ever did anything, again. Bob Fender. Creep! He couldn't get in her pants, and started to spread stories, claiming he had. She saw him on his way home when she was taking the shortcut. She had the knife she carried for safety, and had come up behind him and stabbed him in the back. He fell down, and she stabbed him again and again. She had run, then. She was all covered in blood. She actually had an orgasm, that time! The idiot police said it was a gang killing. Like he had the guts to be in a gang! Come back to this planet!

Then here. Hell, it was so easy! Why not use a talent, if you have it?

Who else?

Nobody had better ever insult her again. Never condescend or get that holier-than-thou attitude with her. She knew how to put a quick end to that crap!

What about those natives who begged every time she went to town? Really, now! Wouldn't the world be better off without them?

She would have to think of different ways to do it. She read all over the place where a MO, they called it, would eventually trip you up.

So change the MO, stupid!

This was going to be the start of a great year. She could feel it!

Martin Zayle was damned worried about this one. He didn't have the resources they had on CSI or any of those big city places. He could probably find what he needed with the fancy equipment, but he had a Sherlock Holmes hand magnifying glass laboratory.

He wasn't going to be able to get enough hard evidence to arrest her, much less for a conviction. If Ken sentenced her to anything, she would go to the main island, and get released.

She was an obsessive paranoid nutcase, and homicidal, with it. She would go on killing. They would eventually get her, but how many more would she kill before they did? How many had she already killed that they didn't know about?

She had to be stopped. If he had to walk up to her on the street and blow her head off, he'd do it, and take his breaks.

He would have to protect Wendy. She was a good woman, who was willing to lend a helping hand to anyone, even people she didn't like. It was his job to protect everyone on the island. He'd sworn an oath to do so. He wouldn't lapse for a second from that oath. Whatever it took was whatever it took.

Marty Feldman had a cold knot in his stomach. Somebody was killing people. No one had a right to kill someone just because they were annoying. That was so far off the track there was no way back. Someone had to be stopped. It was between Wanda and Sandi, in his mind. Sandi would be capable, but would Wanda?

You never knew what a given individual was capable of. This was someone who was, to his way of thinking, insane. That changed the whole equation. This was someone who would go on killing. He didn't know what tripped their switch, so he was as much a likely candidate as anyone for being murdered. He could hope to survive long enough for Wanda to kill Sandi, or vice versa. The one who stayed alive would be the killer.

He pulled into his drive, and stopped, in the carport. He cut the ignition, then sat to think before going inside.

Whichever one survived would be the maniac. If he was still alive, would he have the nerve to end the killing?

He wasn't sure. It was one thing to consider an action, and another to do it.

His inside phone was ringing. He went in to have his friend, Doc, tell him that Wanda was dead.

So! Now it was action or...?

Sandi got out of her car, and went inside. She was going to make plans. It had been a day since Wanda and her anticipation for Martin Zayle to come calling wasn't realized. She had decided she would string him along. He would be her adversary who would make the game worth playing. It wouldn't be any fun without someone to outsmart. Maybe she'd leave him clues to taunt him.

She went into the kitchen with her groceries. She put the meat in the 'Fridge and the canned goods in the cabinet.

At least, she didn't lock her cabinets the way that Wendy idiot did. If she locked them she wouldn't put the keys somewhere, them tell everyone in the neighborhood where they were! Stupid as dirt!

It was hot. She was sweating, and would smell like a pig, if she didn't get a good cool shower. Arthur would be back from St. Martins today, and she wanted to be the nice clean sweet sugarplum for him.

She got in the shower, watered herself down, then reached for the soap. It wasn't there.

Damn! Now she would have to dry off and get the damned soap and start over again!

Someone came into the bathroom door. Arthur must already be home.

"Hon, would you hand me the soap?" she called.

The shadow through the shower curtain came close, and reached in through the slit. She reached for the soap and something hard was put into her hand.

What the hell was th...?

"I got home, and found her in the shower, dead," Arthur Beech wailed. "I don't know what ... the lights wouldn't work, and I could hear the water running, but she didn't answer. I came in, and there she was."

Zayle looked at the short piece of rerod with the wires from two different sockets wrapped around the end. There was a second wire from the same sockets wrapped around the valves in the shower.

"It made a hundred fifty volt circuit that could carry sixty amps. She didn't live ten seconds when she grabbed that rerod. It's a steel shower stall, so it was well-grounded. The shock was enough to run an electric chair!" Doc said.

"Now I really have to wonder," Zayle said. "I thought I had the murders figured. Maybe I didn't. Maybe there's ... someone else."

"I don't know what you mean," Arthur said. "What murders?"

"There were three murders, the last few days," Doc said. He saw Zayle shake his head the least bit.

"But ... what?"

"She didn't figure in any way as a victim of that killer. This shines a new light on the case," Zayle answered. "This was the neatest one. One was cyanide, and two were cut."

"Do you have any idea who's doing it?" Arthur asked.

"Yes, or I did. Maybe it will stop, now. If a killer is doing a serial type of thing, and has the intelligence to change the MO, he knows he'll be caught if he continues. He knows he probably already would be caught if he hadn't changed it."

"Cyanide and stabbing are the same MO, and electricity isn't?"

"The cyanide and stabbings were just garden tools and poisons. Electricity doesn't figure into that. With the personalities involved, it was easy to see how garden tools were a part of the MO, not the particular one chosen," Doc explained. "The killer probably thought it was a different MO, but that has to be figured from a personality standpoint. The real change was electricity. I think I agree with Martin. The killings will stop, now."

"But they may start again when the killer thinks he's gotten away with it?"

"Not if the killer's intelligent enough to know a pause won't be enough to stop the investigation. We'll investigate right through, on this kind of thing. We just have to be realistic enough to know we aren't likely to solve it definitively."

<u>Another Garden Party</u>

Wendy greeted the people as they came to the garden party, one month since the last. She was going to give a talk about orchids. Things had gotten back to normal since Sandi's execution, as she considered it.

She put the big straw purse on the potting bench at the Warren's place, and went to mix and chat before the meeting. She hadn't used the purse in almost a month. She only used it when she was carrying items to use in her speeches, or when she was working somewhere off her property, and had to carry small tools.

Bert and Emily Watkins came to talk about the native Oncidium orchids, and how her showing them how to mount them instead of using pots had made them flourish.

Marty came to embrace her and ask about how the new part of the garden, the cedar copse, was doing. He said he couldn't understand how she could work down there, after what had happened there. She answered that was, hopefully, over and done forever. The past was inalterable. You had to move on. Ed joined them, and said he thought by now that she and Capt. Zayle would be the gossip theme of the month. She replied that he was a wonderful man, and would be a lucky catch for any woman, but she very simply couldn't picture herself the wife of a policeman. She knew, from reading the papers, how difficult it was to live that life.

"You were always more at risk than him!" Ed exclaimed. "It looked like only us members of the garden club were in any great danger! Be logical!"

"What's logic got to do with it?" she answered, with a grin. "That was once, for me, but it would be all the time for him. Too much ... there are nutcases who would shoot a cop for the thrill of shooting a cop."

"In the states. Not here," Marty pointed out.

"It wouldn't work out, for several reasons. I hope to always be a closest friend with him.

"Now! About those orchids!"

"I want to grow cymbidiums, like you do, but they won't survive here, in the tropics," Ed said.

"For god's sake! Don't say that where they can hear you!

"It's a matter of changing several things, not just the temperature. You have to lower the light, and force a rest period. You need something to keep the roots cool. The plant doesn't mean as much to that. You see all that porous rock among them. There's a mister that keeps the rocks damp, without wetting the roots. The evaporation cools the roots. Put your hand down under the foliage, and you can feel the difference."

They chatted for a few minutes, then Emily called the meeting to order. They took care of normal business, then it was Wendy's turn to give her lecture. She went to the little table and put the big straw purse on it.

"The first order is about the native species. This is the tropics, where it rains a lot, but the orchids found here don't like to be wet. That means drainage, which is why they do well mounted, and not so well in pots. They'll do very well in pots for a month or so, then start to decline.

"I brought a few short smooth-barked limbs. Remember that. Smooth-barked limbs don't act like a sponge, and hold water. The plants will coat the limb with roots enough to hold the water they need, and shed the rest.

"The first method, and the best, is Cable-Ties. You place the plant along the mount where it has room to grow, and simply put a couple Cable-Ties to hold the rhizome, when the plant has one, against the bark, then you cut off the unsightly extensions. When the plant had roots around the limb you cut off the rest of the Cable-Tie." She demonstrated with items from the purse, as she spoke, holding the plant and materials where they were clearly visible to her audience.

"Another method is okay, for some. It involves using Super Glue in a couple of small spots. I don't care for that method, personally." She demonstrated.

"Next, string. Make a self-tightening loop knot, and tie the plant like it's with a Cable-Tie. The problem is keeping the plant steady until you get the first one in place.

"Next is with plastic tape. You can use duct tape, or regular adhesive, but remember that water will eventually make them come loose. If the plant roots quickly enough, that is no problem.

"Next is with the (she brought out a roll of electrical tape) ... how did that...? Do *not* use electrical tape. It has oil in the adhesive that orchids do *not* like!

"Let's see. This is a strip of plastic tape that you put one end of on the mount with a thumb tack, pass it across the rhizome, then pull until firm, then put another tack this side, cut the tape roll off, and voila!

"Another method is with electrical cord. You have to be very sure there is no exposed copper, so not many people use it. Copper is deadly to orchids." She wrapped the cord expertly, and reached into the bag to come out with stripping pliers.

"Whatever...? How did that ... oh, I remember. These are opposite of what you need! They strip the plastic *off* of the copper! I must have picked that up when I picked up the cutting pliers. I was in a hurry, and left them on the same board." She brought out cutting pliers to cut the wire. "Be sure the insulation still covers the copper."

"We can sometimes use the larger fence staples. They can over-compress the rhizome, or snap it, so be careful how firmly you tap them into place. I seldom use them, but use the square ones when I do, so as to be able to go around the rhizome.

"Any questions before we go on to the light requirements?"

She finished her speech. They had snacks, and hung around talking about any and everything. The murders were still a main topic. She said it was time to move on. She was personally sure that horrible episode in their lives was over and done with for good.

She drove back home at a little after midnight. She stopped where the road was separated from a drop of a hundred meters to the sea by a low rail. She considered whether she should toss the electrical stripper and cutting pliers over.

She sighed, and got back in her car. What the hell? Nobody would ever connect those things to her and Sandi. Why throw away perfectly good tools? Just make certain they're hung on the rack, where they belong. The only time they could've caused any trouble was right at first, when her usual perfectionism let them *not* be there. It would never be remarkable for them to be there. No one could show those pliers and stripper were ever used in a specific place.

Tomorrow would be time to spray the roses. The future looked bright today, when a few days ago everyone had to wonder if they had any future.

She was personally certain she had acted in the best interest of everyone. She had seen a thing must be done, and she did it.

And no. The next one wouldn't be easier. There would be no next one.

C. D. Moulton's works are available on most major outlets as printed or e-books. CD writes the CD Grimes, PI mysteries, the Det. Lt. Nick Storie mysteries, the Clint Faraday mysteries, the Flight of the Maita science fiction series, books on orchid culture and many others of many types. Mystery, adventure, intrigue, science fiction, fantasy, paranormal, mild erotica, and factual.